ABOUT THE BANK STREET READY-TO-READ SERIES

Seventy years of educational research and innovative teaching have given the Bank Street College of Education the reputation as America's most trusted name in early childhood education.

Because no two children are exactly alike in their development, we have designed the *Bank Street Ready-to-Read* series in three levels to accommodate the individual stages of reading readiness of children ages four through eight.

- ○ *Level 1:* GETTING READY TO READ—read-alouds for children who are taking their first steps toward reading.
- ● *Level 2:* READING TOGETHER—for children who are just beginning to read by themselves but may need a little help.
- ○ *Level 3:* I CAN READ IT MYSELF—for children who can read independently.

Our three levels make it easy to select the books most appropriate for a child's development and enable him or her to grow with the series step by step. The *Bank Street Ready-to-Read* books also overlap and reinforce each other, further encouraging the reading process.

We feel that making reading fun and enjoyable is the single most important thing that you can do to help children become good readers. And we hope you'll be a part of Bank Street's long tradition of learning through sharing.

The Bank Street College of Education

For Julie
—B.B.

To Jono, gift of God
—N.W.

A HORSE CALLED STARFIRE
A Bantam Little Rooster Book
Simultaneous paper-over-board and trade paper editions/April 1990

Little Rooster is a trademark of Bantam Books,
a division of Bantam Doubleday Dell Publishing Group, Inc.

Series graphic design by Alex Jay/Studio J
Associate Editors: Gwendolyn Smith, Gillian Bucky

Special thanks to James A. Levine, Betsy Gould,
and Erin B. Gathrid.

Library of Congress Cataloging-in-Publication Data
Boegehold, Betty Virginia Doyle.
A horse called Starfire / by Betty D. Boegehold ;
illustrated by Neil Waldman.

p. cm. — (Bank Street ready-to-read)
"A Bantam little rooster book."
"A Byron Preiss book."
Summary: Lone Owl and his son Wolf Cub encounter
a horse for the first time.
ISBN 0-553-05861-4. — ISBN 0-553-34853-1 (pbk.)
[1. Horses—Fiction. 2. Indians of North America—Fiction.]
I. Waldman, Neil, ill. II. Title. III. Series.
PZ7.B63572Ho 1990
[E]—dc20

89-37772 CIP AC

Bantam Books are published by Bantam Books, a division of Bantam Doubleday
Dell Publishing Group, Inc. Its trademark, consisting of the words "Bantam Books"
and the portrayal of a rooster, is Registered in U.S. Patent and Trademark Office
and in other countries. Marca Registrada. Bantam Books, 666 Fifth Avenue, New
York, New York 10103.

PRINTED IN THE UNITED STATES OF AMERICA

0 9 8 7 6 5 4 3 2 1

Bank Street Ready-to-Read™

A Horse Called Starfire

by Betty D. Boegehold
Illustrated by Neil Waldman

A Byron Preiss Book

A BANTAM LITTLE ROOSTER BOOK
NEW YORK · TORONTO · LONDON · SYDNEY · AUCKLAND

Contents

Chapter 1
FROM SPAIN

The man from Spain
called his horse Estrella.
She was a golden horse
with a white star
in the middle of her forehead.

Estrella and the man crossed the ocean
on a crowded sailing boat.
They came all the way from Spain
to the New World,
where there were no horses.

With many other men
and many other horses,
Estrella and her man
set out to explore.

They rode across the new land,
for weeks and weeks.
One day, Estrella's man grew sick.
He fell behind the others
and lost his way.

The man knew he was dying.
"I must free Estrella," he said.
He pulled the saddle and bridle
off the golden horse.

Chapter 2
WOLF CUB

Estrella stayed by her man
all day and all night.
But he did not move.
Somehow the horse knew
he would never move again.

Now Estrella was alone
for the first time in her life.
Alone and hungry,
the golden horse moved away
toward a hill
with a patch of dried grass.

Behind that hill Lone Owl stood
with his son Wolf Cub.
It was Wolf Cub's first hunting trip.
He had dreamed for weeks
of returning to camp
with plenty of big game.
But they had hunted all day,
and had taken only
a few small rabbits.

Lone Owl was ready to go home.
"Father," said Wolf Cub,
"let's stay a little longer.
Maybe our luck will change."

Just then they heard something.
Wolf Cub put his ear to the ground.
Yes. It was a big animal,
moving slowly over the hill.

Was it a deer?
Or maybe a bear?
The two hunters waited
with bows and arrows ready.

Chapter 3
A HORSE

"Remember to ask the animal to forgive us," said Lone Owl. "We must always ask this before taking an animal's life."

Then over the hill came Estrella.
Wolf Cub could not believe his eyes.
He had never seen an animal
like this one.
"Father," he whispered, "what is it?"

"Don't move," said Lone Owl.
Estrella lifted her head.
She sniffed the air
and looked straight at them.
Then she moved down the hill.

Wolf Cub and Lone Owl stood
as still as stones.
Estrella walked up to Wolf Cub.
She stopped and bent her head
and softly touched his arm.

The boy was filled with wonder.
This strange animal was not afraid
of him. Slowly he lifted his hand
and patted the animal on the nose.

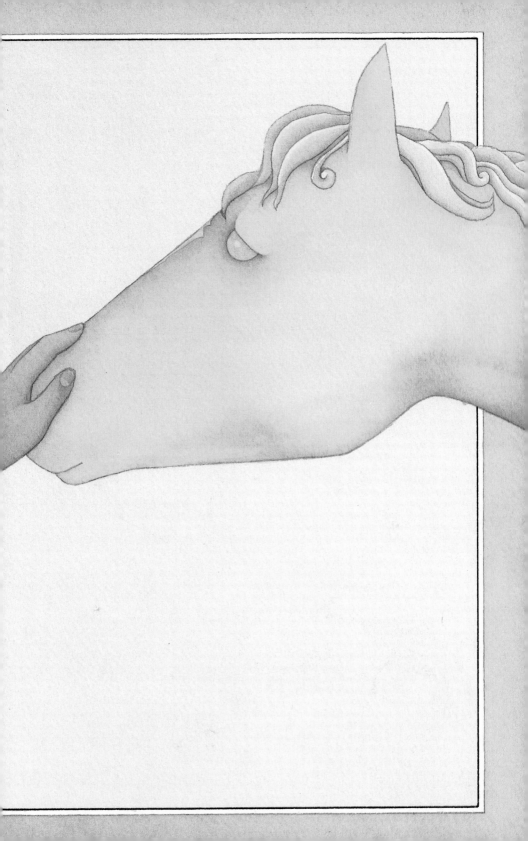

"Father, this is not a wild animal,"
he said.
"This animal is a horse," said Lone Owl.
"I have seen them before.
The paleface men brought them here.
They ride on their horses' backs.
Quick, Wolf Cub. We must hide!
The paleface men may be near."

Lone Owl and Wolf Cub hid
behind a pile of rocks,
where they could watch
without being seen.

Chapter 4
STARFIRE

They waited a long time
while Estrella stayed nearby,
eating grass.
No paleface men came.
At last Lone Owl said,
"A horse would be of great use
to our people. We have never had
such an animal."

"Let me go to her, Father,"
begged Wolf Cub.
"She will not harm me."
Lone Owl watched his son
walk slowly toward the horse.

Lone Owl kept his bow ready,
just in case.
But when Estrella saw Wolf Cub
walking toward her,
she came to meet him.

The boy and the golden horse stood
side by side for a long time.

"See, Father, she is my friend,"
cried Wolf Cub.
"Then you must name her, my son."
"She already has a name,"
said Wolf Cub.
"It is Starfire."

At dawn, Wolf Cub climbed gently
onto Starfire's back.
Lone Owl raised his bow again.
But the horse stood still.
Wolf Cub held on to her long mane.
Starfire began walking slowly forward.

With her head held high,
Starfire carried Wolf Cub
over the hill and
down the long trail
to the place where his people lived.

Lone Owl and Wolf Cub
entered the camp with Starfire.
The whole tribe gathered around them.
Some of the children hid
behind their mothers
when they saw the horse.

The chief stepped forward.
"You have brought us a great gift,"
he said to Wolf Cub.
"The sun, moon, and stars
have smiled on us today."

Betty D. Boegehold is the author of many books for young children, including the popular *Pippa Mouse* series. She has written extensively on child development topics and authored *Getting Ready to Read* in the Bank Street Child Development Series. Ms. Boegehold was a senior editor in the Bank Street Publications Group for over twenty years.

Neil Waldman has worked as an olive farmer, a factory worker, a teacher, and a fruit picker. Since he began his illustration career in 1972, his paintings for book jackets, album covers, and stamps have been widely acclaimed. His book credits include *Bring Back the Deer* and two collections of ghost stories. Neil Waldman lives with his family in Greenburgh, New York.